Specially written for Grandma,
and for my daughters,
Chloé and Audrey.
—*Michelle Nott*

To my niece Ava,
who has a creative mind
and cute face.
—*Nahid Kazemi*

www.enchantedlion.com

First published in 2022 by Enchanted Lion Books,
248 Creamer Street, Studio 4, Brooklyn, NY 11231
Text copyright © 2022 by Michelle Nott
Illustration copyright © 2022 by Nahid Kazemi
Design & layout: Eugenia Mello
All rights reserved under International
& Pan-American Copyright Conventions
A CIP record is on file with the Library of Congress
ISBN 978-1-59270-368-5

Printed in China by RR Donnelley Asia Printing Solutions Ltd.

First Printing

Teddy, let's Go!

Written by **Michelle Nott**
Illustrated by **Nahid Kazemi**

Enchanted Lion Books
NEW YORK

The wavy-haired woman with love in her eyes pulled me close and whispered in my ear.

Then she wrapped me up. And I floated.

A sweet smell surrounded me.

"This..." she said,

"is Teddy."

A nose as small as mine rubbed against my cheek.
We were made for each other.

In the beginning, I would wonder what to do.
I often practiced sitting straight and touching
my toes. Back and forth. Back and forth.

Sometimes, soft arms lifted us both high and held us tight.

When the baby drank her milk, my head propped up the bottle.

After she ate her mushy vegetables...

we both had a bath.

We loved holding hands...

and walking by ourselves. Together, we made friends
everywhere we went.

Then it was our first birthday.

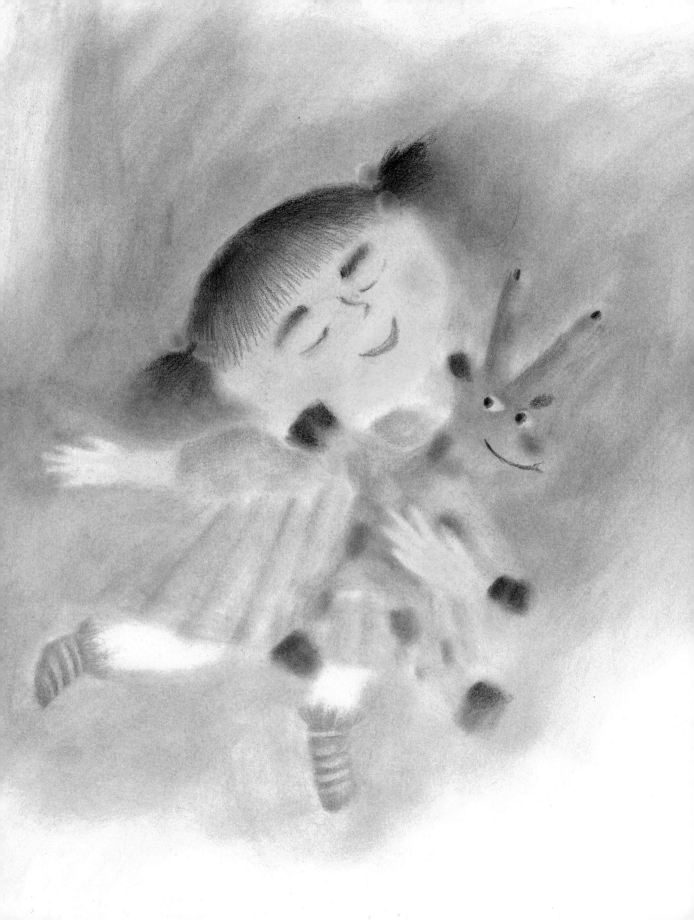

She soon had a name for everything.

"Here's my Rabbit and my Giraffe
and my Teddy and my... my... my..."

So I called her by her favorite word: My.

By the time we were three, My played at school all morning.

The other furry friends and I had tea parties
and wondered what My might be doing.

In the afternoons, My taught me colors and shapes
and how to stack blocks.

At bedtime, My would scoop me up from the rug and wrap both arms around me. This was our moment. I listened for my name.

"Teddy, let's go!"

One summer, I climbed into My's backpack,
and we rode a bus to camp.

When My marched into the woods, I guarded the cabin.

I was wondering what else I should do when...

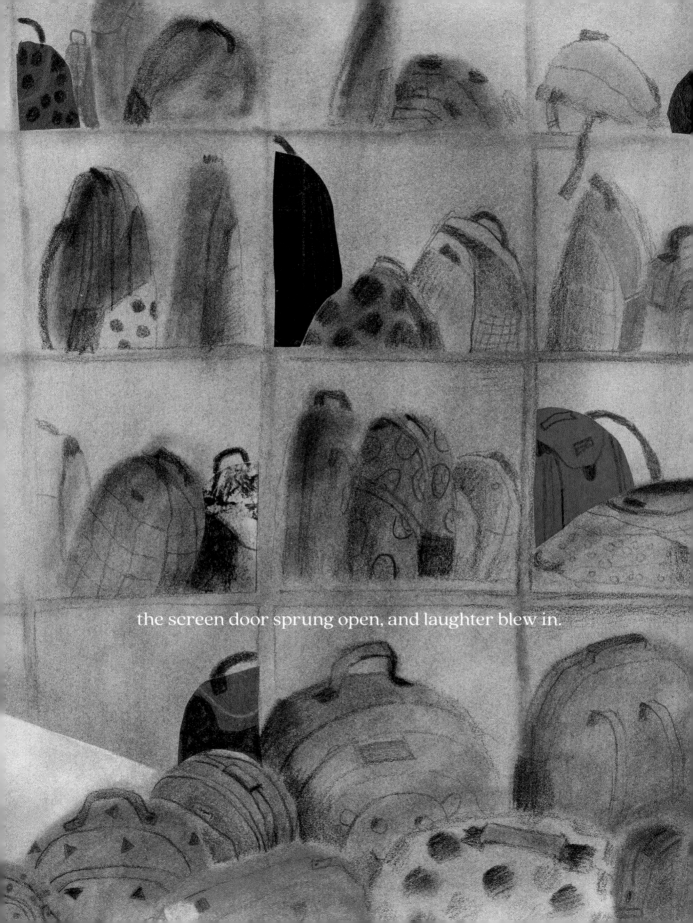

the screen door sprung open, and laughter blew in.

I listened...

"Teddy, let's go!"

That night, her mother drove us home.

My's dad carried her out of the car. I pressed my paws
against the window until morning.

Back in the house, I hiked to the top of her dresser.
Rains came and went, came and went, and I scanned
the room for Rabbit.

One day, My slammed a drawer so hard that I lost my
balance. While I was on the floor, I found Giraffe.

Some days I didn't see much of My.
But when she noticed me alone, she always
reminded me how strong I was and
how high and far I could go.

And when it was time to settle down, I listened...

"Teddy, let's go!"

On our seventh birthday, we laughed
and told each other secrets,
and I whispered happy dreams in her ear.

Then the sun rose and set, rose and set.
Clouds gathered and parted.
Stars glittered across the night sky.

Something felt different.

All the while, I listened...

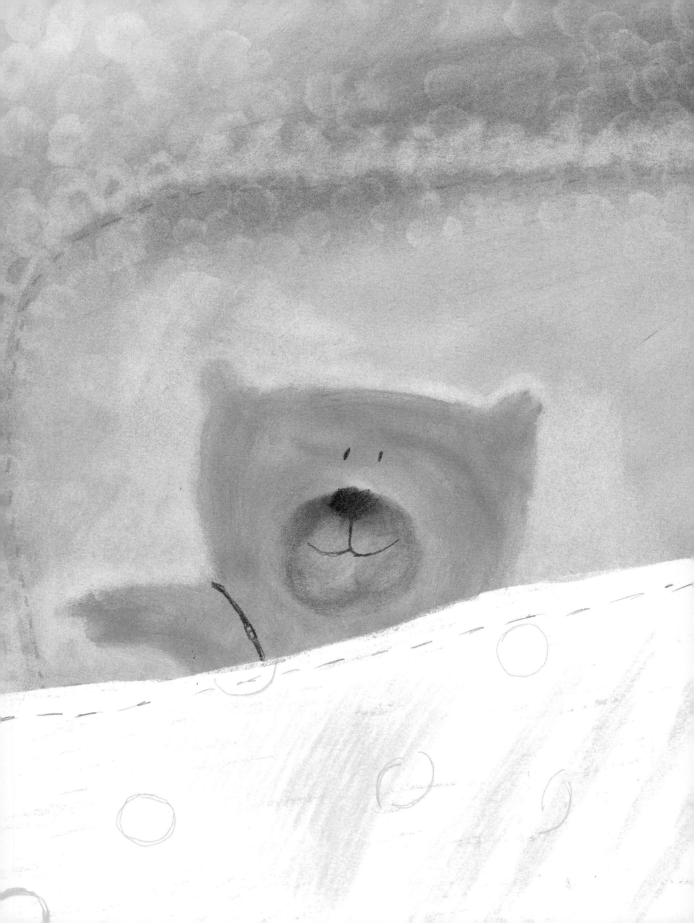

A small voice cried.
My went still.

I stretched out my arms and legs
so My would know I was still there.
She rubbed my paw. I held on and listened...

Her heart beat against my chest all the way to the bathroom.
Then, I let go. She scrubbed me with a cloth.
We wiped the bubbles off my belly.

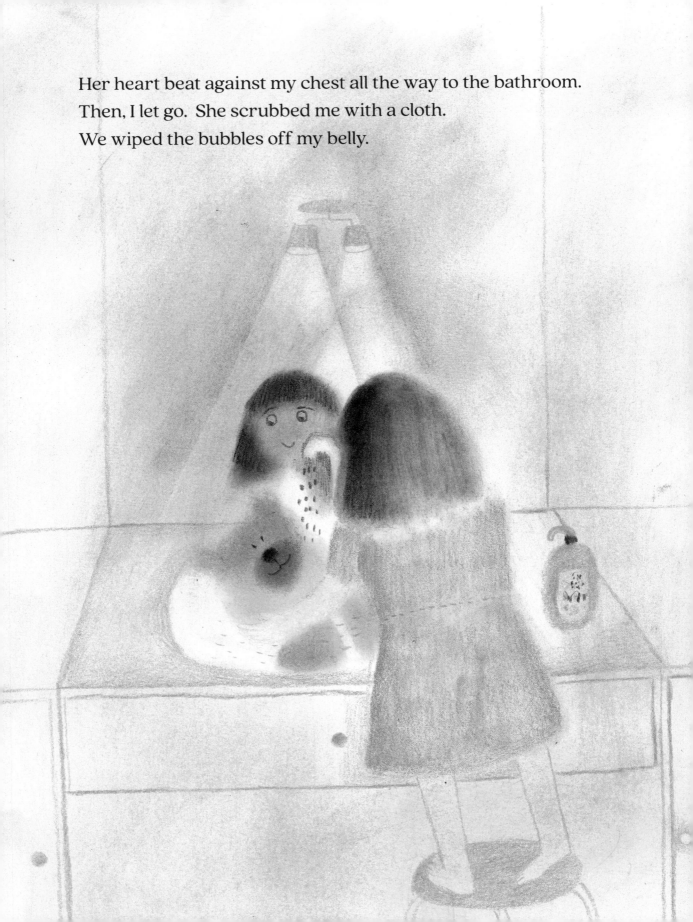

She tucked in some loose fluff and sewed me up.
And I listened...

"Teddy, let's go!"

My and I closed one door...

and opened another.

"This..." she said,

"is Teddy."

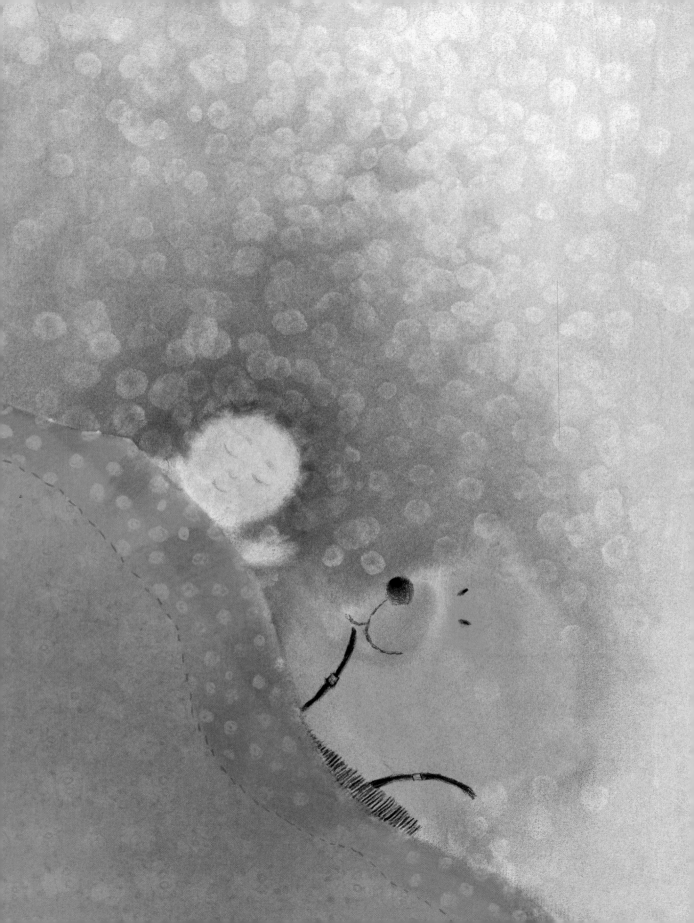

I floated down to our first bed and to a new baby.
This was our moment.

I listened... and whispered happy dreams in his ear.